RITE OF PASSAGE

Jeff Coleman

PALLID VISIONS™

Published internationally by Pallid Visions®
PO box 5943
Buena Park, CA 90622
United States

Cover design by Tri Widyatmaka. Cover and interior art ©2017 Lauren K. Cannon. For more information about her work, visit her homepage: http://navate.com/

This book is a work of fiction. Any similarity between the characters and situations within its pages and places or persons, living or dead, is unintentional and coincidental.

For more information about the author, visit his homepage:
https://blog.jeffcolemanwrites.com/

ISBN 978-1-945997-04-4 (Kindle)
ISBN 978-1-945997-05-1 (ePub)
ISBN 978-1-945997-06-8 (Hardback)

Library of Congress Control Number: 2017919157

Acknowledgments

To everyone who's been, at one time or another, an important part of my life: There's only so much space in this book, and it would take at least a book of its own (maybe two) to list everyone deserving of a mention. You are not (and will never be) forgotten.

To my critique group: You guys have helped me so much in my efforts to become a better writer. You always challenge me to see the flaws I wouldn't have spotted on my own, and my stories are stronger because of it.

To Kevin (aka "K1"): You introduced me to the world of indie publishing and encouraged me to pursue it. If you hadn't done so, this book probably wouldn't exist.

To Mom and Dad: You raised me in love and encouraged me to pursue my dreams. This book is the result.

To Win: God heard all of my prayers for the "ideal" wife and sent me someone so much better. Your ever present love and support uplifts me and helps me to be the man I always wanted to be. I love you.

And finally, to all my patrons: You will never know how profoundly grateful I am for your constant encouragement and support. I love you guys! If you became a patron after October 31, 2017, I'm sorry I wasn't able to list you here. But know that you, too, hold a special place in my heart, and that this book wouldn't have been possible without you.

Anthony Colannino	Voni Colannino	Robert Peirson
Jeannine Cook-Battles	JonBoy Maddron	Cassie Ehrenberg
Jenn Vaughn	Monica A. Franklin	Lisa Plante
Buffy Kennedy	Karen Sutton	Jill Babbs
Suzie Queen	Melody LeBeau	Chad Walker
Janis Chandler	Jewelz Lehman	Pat Williamson
Vickie Bracken	Anna Garcia-Centner	Thom Millman
Justin Cooper	Allen Morris	Andi Graham

Christyne Demos	Karen Palumar	Caitlin Peterson
Amy King	Jessica Parkko	Richelle Guilbault
Melissa Holtsclaw	Nick Boyd	Julia Davis

1.

H E SEES THE BOY, pumping his legs as he soars through the air on a swing, and he almost smiles. How carefree and innocent the boy is, not yet aware of the world's cruel designs. His own childhood is a distant thing, far removed from who and what he is today.

The boy releases the chains. He leans forward, and when the swing is at its apex, he slips from the seat. He hurtles through the air, lands on his hands and knees, and grins.

Play. It's a concept he's thought about a lot. In the small hours of the night, when he lays awake unable to sleep, he stares beyond the ceiling, pondering its manifold mysteries. The imagination of a child, he thinks, is a thing of boundless possibilities, a grasp toward the infinite, an exploration of a vast, unformed world filled with all the things that might yet be. It is an art, he thinks, a special kind of magic that he lost the moment he was Changed.

He brushes the thought aside. There will be time for reflection later. Right now, he's focused on the boy. He stares at him from behind a broad oak tree, shrouded in shadow.

Today, the boy will be his.

2.

His name is Gol. He is not an ogre or a troll, a gnome, a fairy or a centaur. There are no stories written of his kind. To the best of his knowledge, he's the only one of his kind. He was once human like the boy, but he is human no longer.

He is the latest incarnation of an ancient lineage, a succession stretching back beyond the foundation of the world. He cannot reproduce, but like humans he's compelled to propagate, to continue the work of his ancestors. Though he's lived for thousands of years, has witnessed the rise and fall of long-forgotten civilizations, in the end, like all living things, he too must die.

He's spent a great deal of time pondering his origins. The memories of his ancestors are a part of him, but they're so numerous and convoluted by the ravages of time that the secrets of the distant past remain shrouded in mystery. Someday, before the stars have burned up all their hydrogen, before the world is an icy ball of lifeless stone, before the universe is a tepid mass of eternal darkness, he hopes his progeny will solve that riddle, that perhaps they'll even find a way home. But that will be a task for the boy and his descendants.

His own days are nearly at an end.

3.

G OL WAITS FOR THE BOY outside his school. He's kept tabs, has spent most of his afternoons watching from the shadows, studying the boy's routine. He must be careful. In planning for this day, he consulted the collective memories of his ancestors, and he knows that humans don't give up their offspring easily.

He leans against the oak, shaded by the branches and the leaves, his skin the color of the bark, and he watches as one by one, the other children filter out of the playground. The boy lingers. Though most of his third grade classmates can't wait to leave, he likes to stay behind and play alone. He prefers the company of his imagination to that of other children, and it is this unique trait, the sign of an introspective mind, that makes him so admirably suited for the continuation of Gol's work.

He watches as the boy tromps around in the otherworldly stillness of the empty playground, transforming the ground before him with his imagination.

Gol is fascinated by the boy's power, and he takes a moment to mourn him and the world he's about to lose.

He leans against the oak, shaded by the branches and the leaves, his skin the color of the bark.

4.

JAMES STANDS TALL and proud atop the dizzying heights of the cylindrical monkey bars. From there he surveys the whole of his kingdom, silent and peaceful. He watches the peasants who are hard at work in the fields, harvesting wheat. He moves on to the sandy dunes of the distant desert, briefly considers a pilgrimage through the swirling sands.

The wind tugs at the corners of his robes so that they flap majestically, and he thinks that it's good to be king.

Eventually he climbs down, careful to avoid scraping his hands and knees, and he leads an invisible procession toward the swings.

The instant he sits down he's an astronaut blasting off into space, absorbed by the colossal momentum of the rocket packs as they rumble and burn, sending him soaring toward the stars. But something goes wrong. A light beeps on his center console. There's been a leak, he realizes, and his oxygen levels have gone critical. He has no choice but to abandon ship. He sucks in a gulp of air and holds his breath, wondering if the desperate gesture will sustain him, and he jumps, out of the swing, through the stars, and plummets back to Earth.

He brushes himself off, dons his royal robes once again and moves on toward the old oak, intrigued by recent rumors of buried treasure.

James hears a sound.

He stops.

Turns.

Looks over his shoulder.

Suddenly the playground is filled with sinister shadows. He gets ready to run, and that's when he feels something grab his shoulder.

James opens his mouth to scream, but before any sound can escape his lips the figure behind him has covered his mouth. Whoever he is, he's wet and smells of rot and decay. James's eyes bulge and he gags from the stench. He chomps down hard, hoping to be released, and his teeth tear deep into a sinewy mass. But it makes no difference. The thing over his mouth does not move, not an inch, and before James knows what's happening he's falling, tumbling, down into the Earth. He watches as the light of the sun recedes, transfigures into a tiny solitary star in an ocean of black, and that's when he realizes it's difficult to breathe.

5.

GOL SEES THE BOY COMING. He turns his head to make sure no one's watching, first in one direction then the other. When the boy is standing beside him he grabs him, covering his mouth so that he can't scream. The boy bites, but it does not hurt.

He opens one of the many hidden entrances to his home, and he and the boy slide down together, pulled by gravity through a narrow loamy tube. They fall through the bowels of the Earth, through layer upon layer of fossilized plants and animals, each only a footnote in the history of the world.

Eventually, the Earth opens. He positions himself, holds the boy close to make sure he's secure, and when they finally land in a broad stone antechamber illuminated dimly but evenly by a light source unknown even to Gol, he bends his knees and braces for impact.

He lands in a low crouch, the boy positioned safely in the crook of his arms. He rises to his feet, takes a moment to find his balance and glances down. The boy's eyes are closed and he's breathing shallowly. Gol sets him down on the rough stone floor and waits for him to wake.

6.

MEMORY COMES SLOWLY. James's eyes flutter, and at first he thinks he's emerging from a bad dream. In that moment, he's sure his mom will call him down to the kitchen and tell him breakfast is ready. Then he feels the hard surface beneath his back that's so unlike his comfortable mattress at home.

He comes fully awake then. He leaps to his feet, ignores the dull pain radiating from the small of his back, and when he turns, sitting across from him is a creature only vaguely resembling a man.

In the dim light, he can tell that the creature is old. He has brown leathery skin caked with dirt and pebbles. A monster.

James shrieks and stumbles back until he bumps into the wall and can stumble no further.

"You're awake." The creature's voice is low, gravelly.

"Don't hurt me," James begs, and he starts to cry. "Please, don't hurt me."

"What's your name?"

"Mom says not to talk to strangers." James says this as if the words are a talisman that will protect him from harm.

The creature gazes at him for a moment without answering. Eventually he shrugs, gets up and begins to walk away.

"I want to go home!" shouts James, and a dozen other Jameses echo their protests beyond the chamber. "Take me home!"

The creature sighs. "I have work to do." He turns away. He reaches for the handle of a massive metal door, opens it and is about to step through.

"Wait!" cries James, "Come back!" But the creature is already gone.

In the dim light, he can tell that the creature is old. He has brown leathery skin caked with dirt and pebbles. A monster.

7.

GOL IS IN HIS STUDY. It is another room carved into the bowels of the Earth, one of millions. He sits on a chair of stone, holds in his right hand a thick leather-bound volume in a language that was ancient when the world was new. But he isn't paying attention to the words. Instead, he's thinking about the boy.

Why does he feel guilty? The emotion gnaws at him. He did what had to be done. The lineage must not die with him. It is imperative that the work of his ancestors continue, even if he himself cannot remember why. Reverently, he gazes down at the book in his hands. His home is littered with books of all kinds, books from every race and every age, histories, stories, treatises on science and math, magic, religion and mysticism. But there is no book more important than this one.

Contained within its hundreds of pages is the Rite of Passage, the means by which he was reborn, the means by which the boy will also be reborn. It is a complex ritual of arcane powers designed to induce change. It is a conjuring of entities not entirely living, entities whose names have been lost through the ages to all but he and his ancestors.

Gol remembers through their eyes the hundreds of humans who were sacrificed when they first attempted the Change, humans who suffered and, if they were very lucky, eventually died, all so that this book could be written to instruct future generations.

His master, the one who came before him, taught him the ritual just after Gol's own Changing, and he's been studying it ever since. He knows the contents backwards and forwards, yet now that the time has finally come, he finds he's still nervous and unsure.

13

Gol thinks of the boy again, and he realizes it's been a few hours since they arrived. The boy must be hungry and thirsty. Gol decides to fetch food and water.

He sets the book aside, places it delicately atop a wrought iron desk. Then he glances up, toward one of the many holes connecting him to the outside world. He grabs hold of the stone and the dirt and claws his way to the surface.

8.

JAMES SHIVERS. Wherever he is, it's cold. His stomach is rumbling and his throat is dry. His eyes are red and puffy from crying, though now all he feels is numb and cold.

He hears the shuffle of footsteps. The door opens. He looks up.

In the dim light, he can see the creature standing in the doorway, holding something.

"Food," the creature says, and he throws it down onto the ground beside him.

James stares at it, uncertain. Hunger has turned him inside out, but still he hesitates.

"Meat," the creature clarifies. "It's cooked."

The creature sets a pitcher down as well, and motions for James to drink. This James takes and gulps greedily. Water. It reconstitutes the tissues at the back of his throat. It feels cool and smooth going down.

"What's your name?" asks the creature.

James just looks at him, too scared to speak.

"Gol," says the creature, and he gestures to himself with a large stumpy hand.

"I want to go home," says James by way of reply.

The creature doesn't respond.

"Where am I?"

"Home," says the creature.

"This isn't my home," argues James.

Again, the creature says nothing.

A crushing weight settles onto James's chest, and he finds it hard to breathe again. He wants his mom, his dad, even his annoying little brother who always steals his iPod and hits him when his parents aren't watching.

"Eat," says the creature, and he gestures at the cooked carcass lying on the floor.

James considers it. His stomach is crying out for food. But he's too frightened, too scared he'll never see his family again.

The creature begins to move, and James bolts from the floor, again backing into the stone wall.

"Leave me alone," he says. "Stay away from me."

"I won't hurt you," says the creature, but James doesn't believe him. On TV, the bad guys always say that before they kill you.

Finally, the creature slumps his shoulders and heads back to the door.

9.

G OL IS STANDING IN the middle of a rocky desert, nestled deep in the heart of a narrow valley. It is one of the many places accessible to him through the network of tunnels built by him and his ancestors. He is standing before a brass mechanical instrument covered with knobs and wheels and filled with lenses and mirrors. It is a telescope, though it is not like any telescope the humans have seen. He places an eye near the bottom and gazes into the heavens.

He likes the desert. The nights are dark—without light pollution, he can see the whole of the Milky Way, spread before him in the sky like dust—and the location is remote. Humans rarely venture out this far, and when they do, Gol always has plenty of time to hide.

He turns one of the knobs, and the device moves a fraction of a degree to the left. He stares at the celestial canvas above, commits the sight to memory, then moves the telescope another fraction of a degree.

When he is done, he will return to his study and draw a diagram. And when he's drawn his diagram, he'll compare it to all the other diagrams that he and his ancestors have made in search of patterns. He doesn't know precisely what he's looking for, but he knows that when enough data has been collected, he, or his descendants, will piece together a solution.

He gets ready to move the telescope, then pauses and realizes he wasn't paying attention. Irritated, he returns to the eyepiece and looks again. Any other day, with his quick and exceptionally detailed memory, he'd have finished hours ago. But today he's distracted.

Every time he sees the stars, he's reminded of his Changing, and every time he's reminded of his Changing, he's inevitably reminded of the boy.

The boy was happy before Gol took him. Will he be happy after the Rite of Passage? Gol ponders if he himself is happy now and comes up short.

Perhaps he should talk to the boy. He can't tell him what he's going to do—some of his ancestors had tried to be honest about their intentions, and the Rite had always proven exceptionally difficult as a result—but he can prepare the boy as best he can, at the very least try to comfort him, if such a thing is possible.

Satisfied for the time being, he shrugs thoughts of the boy aside and returns his attention to the stars. There is important data to collect.

He is standing before a brass mechanical instrument covered with knobs and wheels and filled with lenses and mirrors.

10.

Ｊ AMES HAS TRAVELED back and forth, between the waking world and the world of dreams. The line between the two has blurred, morphed into something murky and unrecognizable. Visions of his brother and his parents dance before his eyes, beckoning to him from beyond the walls, calling for him to return home. He tries to follow their voices, only to jolt awake on the cold stone floor and discover he's dreaming.

Time no longer holds any meaning. He doesn't know the hour. He doesn't even know the day of the week. All he knows is the hardness of the stone beneath his back and the strangeness of the semi-darkness before his eyes.

At first, when he hears the creature's voice, he thinks it's a hallucination. Only when the sound doesn't stop does James open his eyes again, and when he sees the creature standing before him, he comes fully awake with a start.

"Boy," the creature whispers, "Are you awake?"

"I want to go home," says James, as if their previous conversation had never ended.

"I know," says the creature, and he sits beside James.

James recoils.

There is a pause, a pregnant moment in time, before the creature speaks again.

"Do you ever wonder what it would be like to be different?"

"What?" James has no idea why the creature is asking him this, and he's too afraid to answer.

"You're just a child," the creature continues. "There are so many things you don't yet understand."

The creature sounds hesitant and unsure. James hasn't heard him speak like this before.

"I myself was taken long ago. Like you, I didn't want to leave my home, my family. But then I became different. I was no longer the child I once was. I understood things differently."

"I don't want to be different," says James. "I want to go home."

"Sometimes we don't have a choice." The creature's voice has dropped almost to a whisper. "Change comes to us all, whether we want it or not. Sometimes," the creature says, "we must make the best of things as they are."

When the creature gets up to leave, James jumps to his feet and shouts after him. "Take me home! Take me home now!"

The creature hangs his head but does not look back.

"Rest," he says over his shoulder. "Tomorrow will be a busy day." Once again, he leaves James alone.

11.

AFTER GOL COMMITS his astronomical observations to paper, he goes to bed. He wants to be well rested for tomorrow. But he can't sleep. Every brush with unconsciousness ushers in the same guilt he felt before. It whispers in his ear, accuses him of a terrible crime.

"I must," he mumbles to himself. "I have no choice."

But the guilt only sneers at him with contempt.

His mind wanders, and he finds that when he lets it wander too far, it begins to replay images of his own life before he was Changed. He'd thought those memories long forgotten, but now they flip through his mind like slides.

He remembers his master snatching him from his father's camp when he was only eight years old. He remembers trying to scream and choking on his master's hand. He remembers the horror, the fear and the despair he felt on realizing that he was never going to see his parents again.

But then he'd been Changed, and his old life had fallen away in the light of something new. In this state, he'd understood his master's actions, even rejoiced in them. He'd resolved to be obedient and to learn so that he could be ready to take his master's place.

The boy will be fine, Gol decides, and with that thought, he sleeps for the remainder of the evening.

12.

G OL RISES EARLY. Though the light underground doesn't change with the hours, his senses tell him that outside, in the world above, dawn has broken.

He lies there in the semi-darkness, contemplates the next few hours with grim determination. He doesn't feel guilty any longer—or at least he's managed to wear the guilt down to a dull uneasiness—but he's having second thoughts about whether or not he himself is ready, whether or not he'll be able to summon all the complex forces necessary to complete the rite.

He only has once chance to get it right. A part of himself, a small but essential part, will be transferred to the boy during the process. If anything goes wrong, if he utters even a single misspoken word, if any of the runes in the Room of Change have been worn away to the point of illegibility, that part of himself will be lost, and the line of succession will die with him.

But he's studied the rite for thousands of years, has pored over every detail in the book, until every word, every syllable, every symbol of that long forgotten language was committed to memory. He's inspected and re-inspected the runes in the Room of Change, an innumerable mass of archaic markings that spatter the chamber like stars, and he knows that nothing has been lost. He shakes uncertainty aside. He will not fail.

Gol takes a deep breath. Holds it. Lets it out slowly, working to reduce the rhythm of his heart. After today, he won't have to worry. He'll remain for a hundred or so years to train the boy, but even should he die prematurely, the boy will still have everything he needs to fulfill his purpose, all of it locked inside his head.

Gol bolts out of bed, suddenly invigorated, eager to be done. Hunger gnaws at his insides, and he climbs into one of the many open holes leading to the surface, where he'll hunt and consume his fill. Just a few more hours, he thinks as he worms his way through the tunnel, and for the first time in centuries, he actually smiles.

13.

A screech. James scrambles to his feet, fully alert. The door to his chamber opens, and he turns to see the creature standing before him on the threshold, face set in a stony stare.

The grisly visage is terrifying, and in one adrenaline-packed moment he decides to bolt, hoping to take the creature by surprise. But the creature scoops him up in one arm before he can break into a sprint, and he finds himself looking down at the floor, kicking and screaming.

"Take me home!" he cries, spittle flying from his lips.

"You'll be home soon," says the creature, and James falls still.

"What?" he asks, sniffling.

"You'll be home soon," repeats the creature.

"Home? You'll take me home?"

"Yes," says the creature after a pause. "I'll take you home."

The creature turns, and James is carted off down a long hallway.

14.

GOL CARRIES THE BOY through the underground palace. He knows the way to the Room of Change by heart, though it's miles away from them and can only be found in the middle of a winding labyrinth of stone and dirt that covers much of the Earth.

He will not feel guilty. What he said to the boy is the truth. After he's Changed, this will be the boy's home.

15.

G OL STOPS BEFORE A massive iron gate.
The Room of Change.

He bows his head, a sign of reverence to all who came before him, to all who, like him, were brought to this place to be sacrificed before the altar of need. He offers a silent prayer of thanks for what he will accomplish today, and the shriveled up organs inside him flutter in nervous anticipation.

He opens the gate.

Before him lies a massive cavern. The walls and the ceiling beyond shimmer with millions of bright, star-like points, each a unique rune identifying some Being from before the formation of the world. The room is so large, the ceiling so high, it feels like they're outside, surrounded by perpetual night.

The boy exhales loudly but does not say a word.

Gol closes the gate and sets the boy down. He does not move, does not try to get away, for which Gol is grateful. He kneels and closes his eyes. He can feel the souls of his ancestors gazing down on him, as well as looking upon him from within.

Gol is infused with a calm and a peace he hadn't felt a moment ago. The filaments of his soul have aligned, like iron filings before a magnet.

He rises. He gazes down at the boy, who is goggling at the shimmering walls, and scoops him up once again.

He carries him to the center of the room, a sojourn that takes the better part of an hour. At the center is a polished circular platform. Surrounding it are thick stone pillars, reaching up toward the celestial dome that hovers far above, out of sight. At the center of the platform is a disk, propped at a forty-five degree angle. Attached to the disk are four iron manacles.

Gol carries the boy to the platform. It isn't until he attaches the first manacle to the boy's left hand that the boy comes alive again. He screams, shouts at Gol. He accuses Gol of lying, begs him not to hurt him. Gol tries to hush him—the sound disturbs the sacred silence of the place, and though the boy's protests are expected, he does not wish for them to continue—but the boy kicks and thrashes even after his arms and legs have been secured.

Gol steps back from the platform and does his best to ignore the noise. He goes to the smaller platform beside it, a much more ordinary outcrop of stone with no adornments save for three large symbols carved into the edge and spaced equally apart. He steps onto it, and all at once he can feel the energy of the chamber focus on him. The memories of his ancestors swirl, coalesce, condense, and for a moment he can almost glimpse their long-held secrets. But he knows that's not what he has come for, that he must attend to the boy.

He closes his eyes—lights in colors Gol has never seen stream beneath the darkness of his eyelids like ribbons—and he begins to speak.

Before him lies a massive cavern. The walls and the ceiling beyond shimmer with millions of bright, star-like points, each a unique rune identifying some Being from before the formation of the world. The room is so large, the ceiling so high, it feels like they're outside, surrounded by perpetual night.

16.

As soon as James passes through the gate, he realizes he's outside. Stars twinkle all around him in such variety and number that he is awed into silence. He doesn't protest as the creature carries him forward.

I'm outside. He's taking me home. The thought brings James some peace. The nightmare will be over soon.

James loses himself in the stars. They are like nothing he's ever seen before. They feel alive. He seems to hear each one, whispering in a language he's never heard yet is quite certain he can understand. They call him by name, beg him to be still, insist that all of this will be over soon.

It isn't until he feels the tight embrace of cold metal around his left arm that he realizes he's been betrayed. His attention snaps to the creature, who's fastening his arms to some kind of stone wall, and he screams.

"Liar!" he spits. "You're a liar! You said you'd take me home. You said!"

The creature presses him into the wall.

"You said!" James repeats, desperate and afraid. "You said you would take me home! Please, don't hurt me!"

"Quiet," urges the creature, but James does not listen. He will not be quiet. He will shout as loud as he can. Hopefully someone will hear him and come to his rescue. He'll make the whole world listen if he has to.

The creature steps away and the boy shouts after him.

"Come back!" he cries. "Let me go!"

The creature steps up onto a platform beside him. He closes his eyes and he begins to speak.

The sound is quiet at first, nearly inaudible against James's desperate pleas. But it soon grows in volume and intensity. James trails off. The creature's voice transfigures, becomes a low resonant rumble beyond the range of human hearing, and instead James begins to sense it with a different kind of hearing. The stars above flood his vision. They begin to echo the creature's words. James is swallowed by a searing white-hot light.

He can hear other voices now, thousands of them. More. They speak as one. White gives way to true stars, and the cosmos and their eternal secrets are opened to him. James—no, that is not his name any longer—is one with them, and they are one with him. They call him, lead him, and he follows, through space, through time, all the way back to the infinitely hot, infinitely dense singularity of the Big Bang and what lies beyond.

His insides warm and something begins to change. The voices speak to various parts of him, instructing his body, his mind, his soul. They command him to transfigure before them, and bound by a code of laws older than the universe, he cannot resist.

A flicker. He is Gol.

A flicker. He is Gol's master.

Flicker.

Flicker.

Flicker.

In an instant that transcends time, he has been each and every one of his predecessors, stretching back to the beginning, stretching back to the birth of the world, the birth of the universe. He is one of them now.

James, his old identity, is still a part of him, but it no longer defines him. He is no longer a child. He is no longer a king. He is no longer an astronaut. He is something greater. He will always remember, but he will never be the same.

The light disappears, and he feels himself spinning, tumbling, down into the dark. The stars recede in a direction perpendicular to length, width, height and time, until blackness has swallowed him whole.

17.

T HE CREATURE WHO IS no longer a boy, whose name is no longer James, is bound before Gol, his eyes closed. Gol can sense his absence. It'll take time for him to wake. He unshackles the body from the altar and lays it down on the stone floor. His skin is now the color of bark, though it is smoother and more pliable than Gol's. He is a part of Gol now, and Gol is a part of him. Gol can feel his soul reaching, searching for its name, and he closes his mind for a time, for one's naming is a private encounter.

For now, he sits beside the body and waits for it to rouse.

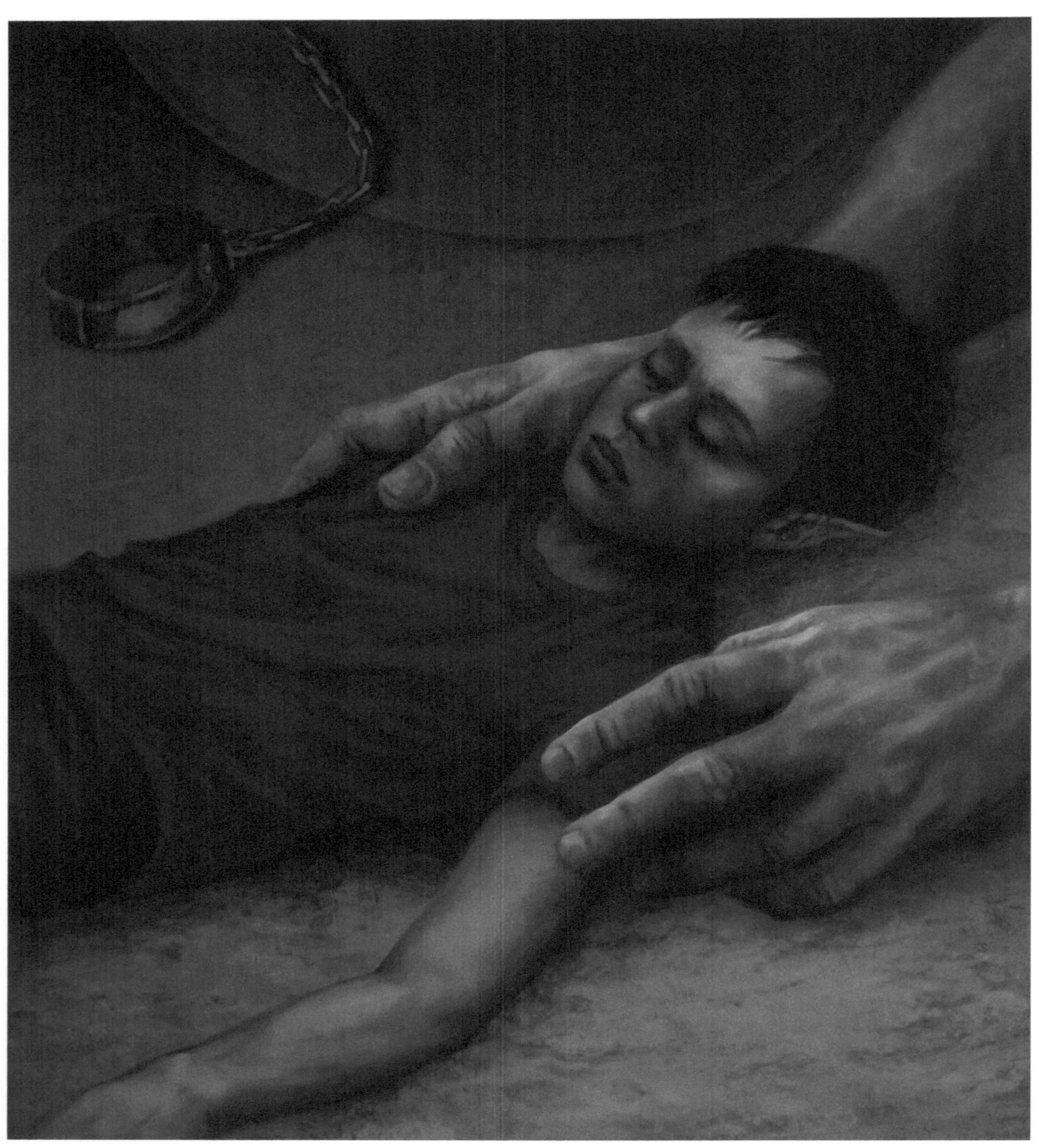

He unshackles the body from the altar and lays it down on the stone floor.

18.

HE IS WANDERING.
Searching.
Reaching.
It's out there, somewhere. His name.
He strains his ears to hear.
After one interminable length of something like time, the universe speaks.
Roegthol.
He embraces his name, absorbs it into himself.
His transformation is complete.

19.

"I AM HOME." It is the first thing he says when he awakes.
"Yes," says Gol, "You are. What is your name?"
"Roegthol," he answers. "I am Roegthol."
"Can you stand?" asks Gol.
"Yes, Father."

Gol waits for him to find his footing. When Roegthol, his child, is finally standing, Gol holds his hand, gives it a gentle squeeze.

"Come," says Gol, and he leads his son back toward the iron gate. Roegthol will not see the gate again until he is much older, and when that time comes he will be alone.

About the author

Jeff Coleman's passion for storytelling goes all the way back to third grade, when he wrote his first (not very good) short story about a leprechaun who enjoys eating green food. While growing up, he was captivated by classic Nintendo games like Zelda, and later computer games like Myst, each of which took place in worlds very unlike our own, and set his imagination aflame with possibilities for his own tales.

During his college years, Jeff fell in love with math, physics and philosophy, subjects that seeded his heart with a profound interest in the many extraordinary mysteries to be found in apparently ordinary things. Jeff is a firm believer that there is more to the universe than immediate appearances suggest, that there is more to our existence than meets the eye. He's therefore fascinated by stories which probe beyond surface observations, stories which attempt to explore the strange and preternatural, stories which unsettle us, which make us think, which make us question what we are and why we're here.

Some of his favorite books are "The Dark Tower," by Stephen King; "Neverwhere" and "American Gods," by Neil Gaiman; "The Night Circus," by Erin Morgenstern; "The Golem and the Jinni," by Helene Wecker; and "Harry Potter," by J.K. Rowling.